Ebb and Flo
and Their New Friend

To Neil, who made it all possible.

Ebb and Flo and Their New Friend
Published by Graffeg Limited 2022.

ISBN 9781802580679

Text and illustrations copyright ©Jane Simmons 1998.
Book design copyright © Graffeg Limited 2022.

First published by Orchard Books 1999.

Awel a Glan a'u Ffrind Newydd (Welsh edition)
ISBN 9781802580686

Teaching Resources
www.graffeg.com/pages/teachers-resources

1 2 3 4 5 6 7 8 9

This book belongs to

_____

_____

_____

_____

Ebb and Flo
and Their New Friend

Jane Simmons

GRAFFEG

Ebb sat in her favourite spot.

Things couldn't be better.

Suddenly, Ebb heard a flapping noise...

...it was a bird, and there it sat in Ebb's favourite spot. Flo giggled. 'Beep, beep, beep,' said the bird.

'Isn't she lovely, Ebb?' said Flo. 'You must share with her. She wants to be friends with you.'

Ebb growled.

'Beep, beep, beep,' said the bird.

That night Ebb did not sleep well.

The days passed, and Ebb got grumpier.

'Look at that bird! Isn't she sweet?' people would say.

'Beep, beep, beep,' said the bird.

'Grrr, grrr,' Ebb growled.

13

Even Granny liked Bird and fed it Ebb's snacks.

'Beep, beep, beep,' said the bird.

Ebb wished Bird would fly far away and
never come back.

The very next morning, Ebb's wish came true.

'Oh no. Bird has gone!' cried Flo.

And when they went out, Ebb had
her favourite spot all to herself.

Things couldn't be better.

Only, Ebb had to eat her dinner
all by herself, and it felt strange
without Bird getting
in the way.

And Ebb found it hard to sleep now that she was alone. It was too quiet without Bird's beeping and her bed was cold and empty.

At Granny's all she could think of was Bird
and she didn't even want her snack.
Ebb wasn't happy at all.

As the long summer days passed, the dragonflies buzzed and the birds sang. Ebb saw some geese on the river...

But none of them swam up close like bird.

'Come on, Ebb,' said Flo. 'Let's go fishing.'

But it was no good. Ebb missed Bird
more than ever.

Then, one day, Ebb heard, 'Beep, beep, beep!'
'Bird!' called Flo.
Ebb barked excitedly.

31

And there Bird sat in Ebb and
Bird's favourite spot...

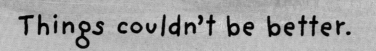

Things couldn't be better.

Ebb and Flo Series

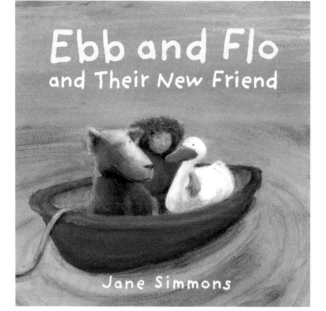

Ebb and Flo and Their New Friend

Jane Simmons

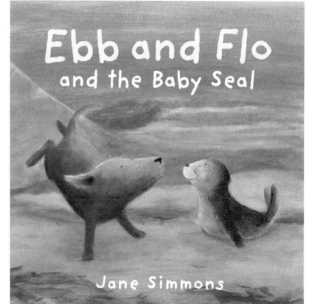

Ebb and Flo and the Baby Seal

Jane Simmons

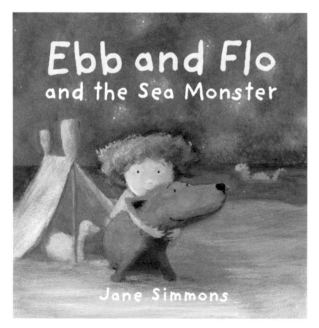

Ebb and Flo and the Sea Monster

Jane Simmons

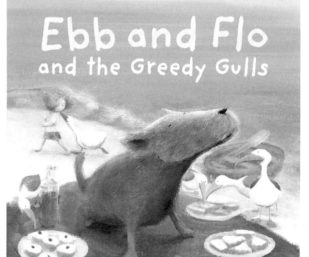

Ebb and Flo and the Greedy Gulls

Jane Simmons

GRAFFEG